Cook it!

illustrated by Georgie Birkett

What's for dinner? Will you help me choose?

What do we need to buy? Let's make a list.

Are we nearly there yet? Not far now.

Look, can you see the shops? There they are.

Lots of vegetables! Which do you like best?

What are those? How many mushrooms?

Can we buy some green olives and cheese?

Phew, this flour is heavy. Hold it tight!

Have we got it all? Put it on the counter.

How much did it cost? Will I get change?

Clean hands! Will you unpack the bags?

Shall we weigh the flour? Is that enough?

Ooh, this feels squishy! It's very messy!

Rolling is hard work. This is a funny shape.

Peep-o! How many slices do we need?

I can cut mushrooms with my toy knife.

Can you spread it out? This smells good.

I've made a face. What shall I put on next?

How long will it take to cook? I can't wait!

Who's home for dinner? Where's my cup?

Who made this pizza? It's really tasty!

Can I have some more? Salad, too?

You're doing a great job clearing up.